21st Century Junior Library

FEELING AND SHOWING EMPATHY

I0877203

Read and Reflect: A Social-Emotional Guide

Emily Rose

Published in the United States of America by:

CHERRY LAKE PRESS
2395 South Huron Parkway, Suite 200, Ann Arbor, Michigan 48104
www.cherrylakepress.com

Reading Adviser: Beth Walker Gambro, MS, Ed., Reading Consultant, Yorkville, IL
Photo Credits: © Prostock-studio/Shutterstock.com, cover, 1; © Monkey Business Images/Shutterstock.com, 5; © wavebreakmedia/Shutterstock.com, 6, 16; © Sergey Novikov/Shutterstock.com, 7; © espies/Shutterstock.com, 9; © Brocreative/Shutterstock.com, 10, 11; © Krakenimages.com/Shutterstock.com, 12; © Mirek kijewski/Shutterstock.com, 13 [top]; © Elena Kharichkina/Shutterstock.com, 13 [bottom, right]; © Abastasiya Aleksandrenko/Shutterstock.com, 13 [bottom, left]; © Lopolo/Shutterstock.com, 14; © Veja/Shutterstock.com, 18; © Prostock-studio/Shutterstock.com, 19; © David Fuentes Prieto/Shutterstock.com, 20 [right]; © mirtmirt/Shutterstock.com, 20 [left]

Copyright © 2022 by Cherry Lake Publishing Group

All rights reserved. No part of this book may be reproduced or utilized in any form or by any means without written permission from the publisher.

Cherry Lake Press is an imprint of Cherry Lake Publishing Group.

Library of Congress Cataloging-in-Publication Data

Names: Rose, Emily (School psychologist), author.
Title: Feeling and showing empathy / by Emily Rose.
Description: Ann Arbor, Michigan : Cherry Lake Publishing, [2022] | Series: Read and reflect: a social-emotional guide | Includes bibliographical references and index. | Audience: Grades 2-3
Identifiers: LCCN 2021036533 (print) | LCCN 2021036534 (ebook) | ISBN 9781534199095 (hardcover) | ISBN 9781668900239 (paperback) | ISBN 9781668906002 (ebook) | ISBN 9781668901687 (pdf)
Subjects: LCSH: Empathy in children–Juvenile literature. | Empathy–Juvenile literature.
Classification: LCC BF723.E67 R67 2022 (print) | LCC BF723.E67 (ebook) | DDC 155.4/1241–dc23
LC record available at https://lccn.loc.gov/2021036533
LC ebook record available at https://lccn.loc.gov/2021036534

Cherry Lake Press would like to acknowledge the work of the Partnership for 21st Century Learning, a Network of Battelle for Kids. Please visit http://www.battelleforkids.org/networks/p21 for more information.

Printed in the United States of America
Corporate Graphics

CHERRY LAKE PRESS

CONTENTS

WHAT IS EMPATHY AND WHAT IS IT GOOD FOR?

Empathy means that you try to understand how someone might be feeling when something sad or bad happens. For example, if your friend tells you that her dog is sick, you can guess that she probably feels sad or worried. Have you ever heard the phrase, "Put yourself in someone else's shoes?" That's an exercise in empathy. When you can

Think about a student in your class who might need empathy. What can you learn by putting yourself in that person's shoes?

imagine or understand how someone else might feel, then you can come up with ways to help them.

If you see that your brother is feeling sad, you might say something nice to him or ask if you can give him a hug.

What is another thing you can say to someone to show empathy?

When was a time you supported a friend?

If you notice your friend is worried about her science test later in the day, encourage her to focus on trying her best. You could also offer to be her study buddy for the next test to boost her **confidence**.

Human beings are wired for **connection**. That means that we are happiest and healthiest when we share our **burdens** and joys with each other. Empathy helps us understand other people's feelings. It encourages us to offer support to help them through hard times or **negative** emotions. Empathy is an example of **emotional** connection, and it can take practice to show empathy.

Think!

Think about a time when you were feeling sad and someone showed you empathy. What did the person do to make you feel better?

What are some things that make you feel happy?

WHEN AND HOW TO SHOW EMPATHY

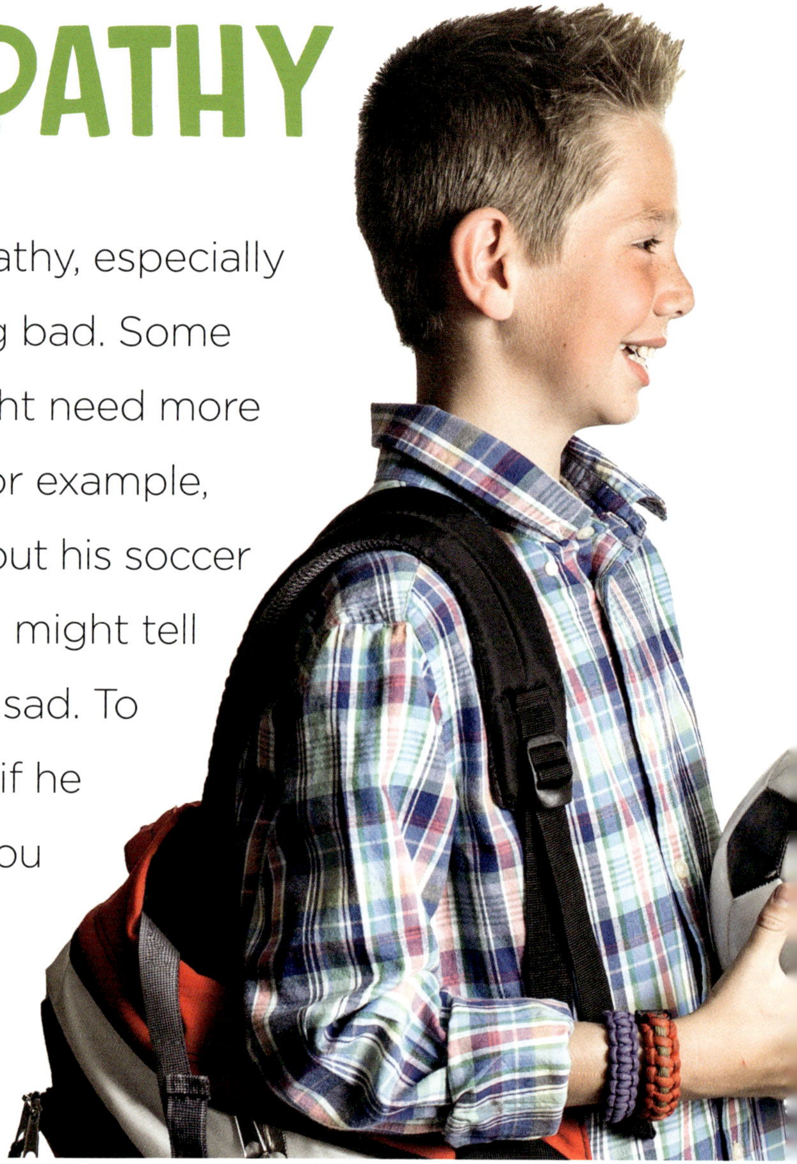

It's kind to show empathy, especially when someone is feeling bad. Some **situations** or people might need more empathy than others. For example, if your friend is **upset** about his soccer team losing a game, you might tell him that it's okay to feel sad. To help him feel better, ask if he wants to practice with you at recess later.

Can you think of a time a pet has cheered you up?

If your friend tells you that her pet fish died, she might be very sad and need empathy for a longer period of time. You can ask her if she wants to tell you her favorite memories about her fish, write her a nice note, or offer to get her a tissue if she feels like she needs to cry.

If you don't know what kind of empathy someone might need, you can ask them. Say something like, "I see that you might be feeling sad. How can I help you?" Then you'll know how to show empathy to your friend, instead of guessing what they might need. Different people like to show or receive empathy in different ways, so asking is always a good idea.

Make a Guess!

Think of a time when you showed empathy to a friend. What did you do for them? How did you know they needed empathy? How did it make them feel?

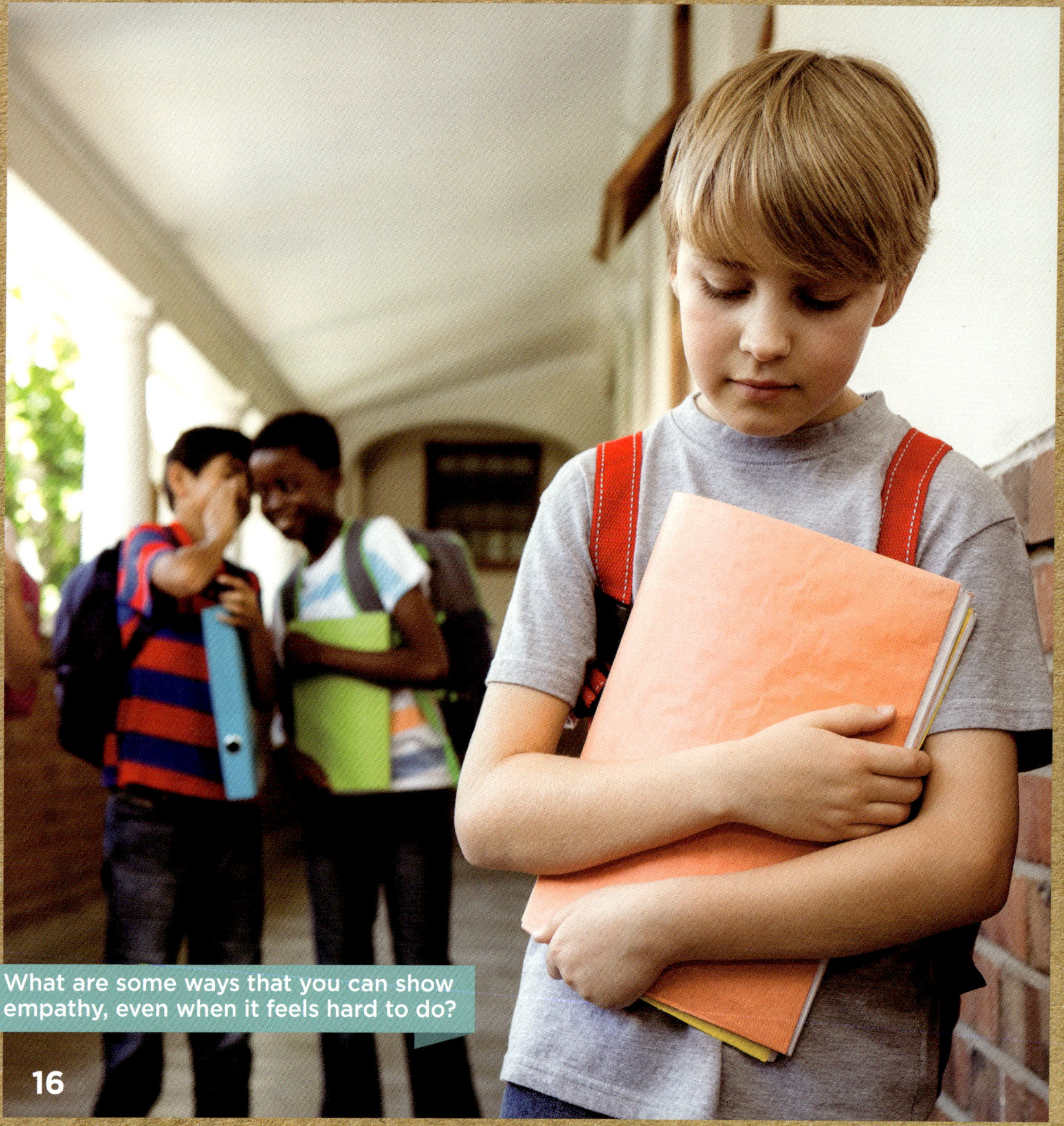

What are some ways that you can show empathy, even when it feels hard to do?

HOW TO SHOW EMPATHY EVEN IF YOU DON'T LIKE SOMEONE

We all have people who are our friends. We also all know people whom we don't get along with as much. Sometimes it feels very hard to show empathy to someone we don't always like. In this situation, remember something called the "Golden Rule." The Golden Rule says to treat others how you want to be treated.

If you feel sad, you want others to treat you with empathy, even if you don't always get along. You can show empathy even when it feels hard. You can tell the person's friend that you noticed the person seems sad. Then the friend can help the sad person feel better.

Can you think of a time you asked someone for help?

Or you can write a nice note and put it in the person's desk, even if you decide not to sign your name on it.

Another way to show empathy is to offer to do something nice for the person. For example, if the teacher asks a boy in your class to pass out papers, but you see that he feels sad, you can offer to pass out the papers instead. That's a nice way to show empathy, even when it feels hard.

Look!

Look back on a time when someone took something "off your plate" and showed you empathy. How did it make you feel?

EXTEND YOUR LEARNING

Imagine a student walks into the classroom stomping his feet and shoving students out of his way to get to his desk. When he gets to his desk, he throws his backpack onto the floor. Everything spills out. Then he crosses his arms and puts his head down on his desk. You can't tell for sure, but you think he is starting to cry a little.

Put yourself in this student's shoes and write about what you might learn. Did you ever feel or act this way in school? What happened that made you feel that way?

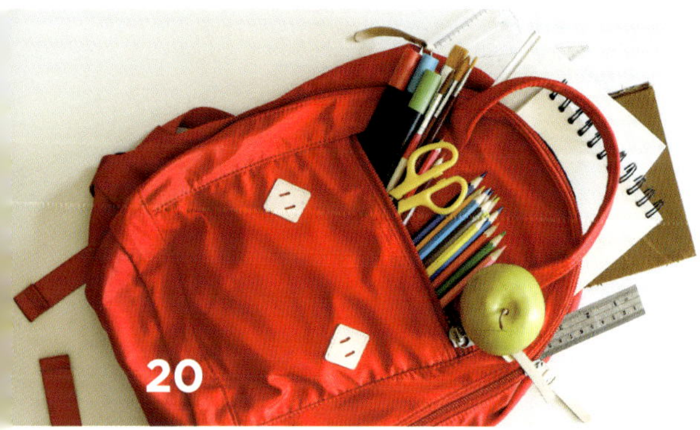

There could be many reasons why this student seems upset. Brainstorm what you think might make someone feel or act this way.

Now that you took time to remember that there are always reasons for someone's **behavior**, how might you help that person feel better? Showing empathy doesn't mean you have to know all the reasons why someone feels the way they do, but it can help to put things into **perspective**.

You can try this exercise anytime you see someone in need of empathy. Think about why they might feel that way and what you can do to help. This idea helps us practice the Golden Rule of treating others how we would like to be treated.

GLOSSARY

behavior (be-HAY-vyuhr) the way you act, the things you do and say

burdens (BUHR-duhns) difficult things that we might carry

confidence (KAHN-fuh-duhns) trust, belief in yourself

connection (kuh-NEK-shuhn) when things are related or joined together

emotional (ih-MOH-shuh-nuhl) having to do with feelings

empathy (EM-puh-thee) to understand how someone might be feeling

negative (NEH-guh-tiv) unfavorable, not positive

perspective (puhr-SPEK-tiv) outlook or viewpoint

situations (sih-chuh-WAY-shuhns) positions you may be in

upset (uhp-SET) to feel disturbed or unhappy

FIND OUT MORE

Books

Sanders, Jayneen. *You, Me and Empathy: Teaching Children about Empathy, Feelings, Kindness, Compassion, Tolerance and Recognising Bullying Behaviours.* Macclesfield, Victoria, Australia: Educate2Empower Publishing, 2017.

Verde, Susan. *I Am Human: A Book of Empathy.* New York, NY: Abrams Books for Young Readers, 2018.

Websites

YouTube—All About Empathy (For Kids!)
https://www.youtube.com/watch?v=Itp21tly8nM
Watch this video to learn what empathy is and why it is important.

YouTube—Communication Skills: Empathetic Listening—*Inside Out*, 2015
https://www.youtube.com/watch?v=t685WM5R6aM
Watch this clip from Pixar's *Inside Out* to see an example of empathetic listening.

INDEX

ABOUT THE AUTHOR

Emily Rose is a school psychologist, yoga teacher, and writer for her mental wellness blog, MissMagnoliaSays.com. She enjoys helping kids and adults understand and manage their emotions and live beautiful lives. Emily lives in Dearborn, Michigan.